# SCRATCH KITTEN
# GOES TO SEA

## JESSICA GREEN • MITCH VANE

LITTLE HARE

www.littleharebooks.com

Little Hare Books
8/21 Mary Street, Surry Hills
NSW 2010 AUSTRALIA

www.littleharebooks.com

*First published in 2008*

National Library of Australia
Cataloguing-in-Publication entry
Green, Jessica.
Scratch Kitten goes to sea.

For primary school age.
ISBN 978 1 921272 44 8 (pbk.).

I. Vane, Mitch.  II. Title.

A823.4

Cover design by Lore Foye
Set in 17/24 pt Bembo by Clinton Ellicott
Printed in China by Imago

5 4 3 2 1

# SCRATCH KITTEN
# GOES TO SEA

# Contents

# 1.

# Scratch Falls Aboard

'You're on your own,' said Maa.
'I'm off to find your Dad. He only
went to fetch a fish, but he's been
gone for weeks.'

Brat mewed. Drat and Flat
squabbled.

Scratch watched two
tomcats fighting over a smelly
fish head.

Maa biffed him on the ear.

'Did you hear me, Scratch?'

Scratch dared not biff her back.
So he biffed Flat instead.

'I'll be away for a while,' said Maa,
'so look out for those boots. You
saw the kick that sailor gave your
brother Splat.'

Scratch yawned and scratched
his neck. Maa biffed him again.
'This is important!' she said. 'People
will let you stick around as long as
you catch mice. And a good fat
mouse is a good cat's dinner. For
the last time now, what are the
hunting rules?'

'Watch. Listen. Wait. And *pounce*!'
sang Brat, Drat and Flat.

Scratch pounced on Maa's tail. Maa biffed him.

'Stay together and behave while I'm gone. And don't go near the ships! Remember, Paa lost his leg on a ship.'

Then Maa stalked away. Brat trailed behind her, yowling. Flat scrambled after Brat.

'But Maa, what if you never come back?' Flat whined.

'What if we get booted into the sea?' yowled Brat.

Scratch padded to the edge of the wharf. 'I'm not staying here with bossy old Drat and Brat,' he thought to himself. 'I want to sail the seas like Paa did, even if he did lose his leg.'

He looked up at a blue sailing ship moored at the wharf. It was called the *Silk'n'Spice*. Sailors were tramping up and down the gangway. They were unloading boxes of china, bales of cloth and sacks of spices.

Scratch swished his tail and twitched his ears. It looked like a bright clean ship. He wondered where it had been and where it was going next. And he wondered what sort of adventures the sailors would have once it sailed. There was only one way to find out.

'I don't care what Maa says,' Scratch said. 'I'm going to sea!'

He sprang onto one of the cables that moored the ship to the pier.

Then he clawed his way along it to
the side of the boat.

'You'll be in trouble, Scratch!' Drat
yowled from the dock.

'I'll tell Maa!' howled Flat.

Scratch took no notice. He
scrambled over the side and landed
on the deck with a thump.

Then he jumped to his feet and washed his paw busily, as if falling aboard was what he had meant to do. After all, a cat must be dignified, even if his ginger fur was scruffy and his tail was a tangle.

He was so busy licking that he didn't notice the *thud-plonk-thud-plonk* sound behind him. Suddenly there was a sharp pain in his tail.

Scratch twisted around, claws at the ready, to see who had trodden on his tail. All he saw was a brown, splintery, wooden leg. Beside it was a skinny, hairy, bare-footed real leg. Towering above Scratch was a thin, stooped, gloomy sailor.

He had big sad eyes and a big red nose. The lower part of his face was covered with ginger whiskers. The top of his head was covered with matted hair that trailed down his back in a scruffy ginger pigtail.

'You great oaf!' Scratch yowled. He puffed out his fur and forced his tail into a bristling brush. Then he lashed out and scratched the splintery leg.

Scratch had the most splendid claws of his litter, but the sailor didn't even squeak. Instead he stooped down and snarled in Scratch's face. 'You foul little flea-bitten moggy,' he said. 'How did you get on board? You think you can take Fluffy's place?'

He snatched Scratch by the scruff and shook him. Then he reached over the ship's rail and dangled Scratch above the water. Scratch twisted wildly, hooked his sharp claws into the sailor's wrist and hung on tight.

The sailor howled. Scratch yowled.

Scratch twisted himself free, clambered onto the sailor's wrist, gave a leap and sailed clear over the sailor's shoulder. His paws hit the deck and he ran, scrambling for the safety of a lifeboat. Underneath the canvas cover were some coils of rope. Scratch hid amongst them.

The sailor stumped away with a toss of his plait, growling threats. Scratch stared after him until he was out of sight, then settled down for a wash to calm his hammering heart. He'd almost been thrown overboard! It was not a good start to sea life.

Maybe things would look better after a nap.

# 2.

# Scratch Finds the Top Spot

Scratch woke up hours later with a fierce pain. He arched up, fur bushy and tail lashing. But it wasn't a sailor trying to hurt him. This time the pain came from his empty stomach.

He peered out at the sailors as they hurried about casting ropes and setting sails. The deck tilted slowly one way, then the other.

There was a creak of timber and a
splashing of water. Scratch edged out
from his hiding place. He crept to a
scupper, stuck his head through and
stared out. All he could see were
waves. And beyond the waves was
sky. No dockyard. No warehouses.
He was at sea!

But being at sea meant Maa was

not there to bring him food. Scratch
would have to find his own. He
sniffed the air. He could smell tar and
salt water and dirty men. He could
also smell food. Keeping his belly
low, he crept along the edge of the
deck until he found a hatch. Then
he climbed down into a dark
passageway.

His nose told him there was something tasty happening ahead, so he followed his nose.

He soon found himself in a dark, hot room with a fire burning on a bed of sand. A bench along one wall was heaped with food. There were onions, potatoes, dried peas and ship's biscuits, and a bowl of oatmeal. There was also fresh fish.

The fish smelled delicious, but there was a problem. The sailor with the wooden leg was at the bench. He was chopping onions and potatoes and tossing them into a huge cooking-pot.

He didn't seem happy. As he chopped the potatoes he grumbled.

As he sliced the onions he moaned.
He stopped chopping to wipe his
eyes, then chopped up the fishes and
threw them at the pot, bones and all.
Pieces of fish fell on the bench.

The peg-leg sailor was dangerous,
but Scratch was so hungry that
for a moment he forgot all about
the danger.

He stared at a little fish on the edge of the bench. He crept closer and closer. Then, quick as a flash, he hooked his claws into the sailor's leg, climbed up it and leapt onto the bench. Peg-leg stumbled backward with a roar as Scratch pounced on the little fish. Potatoes thudded onto the floor. Dried peas scattered everywhere.

The sailor lunged at Scratch. 'Scat, you dratted cat!' he roared. 'Get your scrawny carcass out of my galley or *you'll* be dinner!' He grabbed his chopper. Scratch bit into the fish and jumped from the bench just as the chopper slammed down. Potatoes bounced around Scratch as he darted away to hide under the bench.

Peg-leg crouched and slammed the chopper down again, a whisker length from Scratch's tail. Splinters flew.

'I warned you!' he roared. 'This was Fluffy's galley! Now scoot, or I'll be chopping you up for the stew!'

With the fish still clamped in his jaws, Scratch scooted.

*Thwack!* The chopper bit into the leg of the bench. Scratch leapt back up onto the bench, then jumped to the safety of a broad beam above the bench. It was a safe spot with a clear view of the galley.

Peg-leg climbed to his feet and glared about. He looked up and saw Scratch on the beam.

'How dare you sit up there?' he bellowed. 'That spot was my Fluffy's Top Spot, and it's for champion mousers only!' *Swish, swish*, went the chopper. 'But you're just a good-for-nothing thief!'

Scratch cowered backwards along the beam as the chopper swung. Then Peg-leg dropped the chopper, reached up and grabbed Scratch by the tail. Scratch dug his claws into the beam, but Peg-leg pulled him down and shook him until Scratch's fish fell to the floor. Still holding Scratch by the tail, Peg-leg stumped along the passage to the hatch and hurled him up into the bright sunshine on deck.

# 3.

# Scratch Goes Aloft

It took a long time for Scratch to calm his nerves, but a few hours later he crawled out of his hiding place and sniffed the salty air. No stinking docks. No nagging brothers and sisters. Just the splashing of the waves and the flapping of the sails, the shouting of the sailors, and the cries of the seagulls high above the masts.

There was only one thing wrong.
He was even hungrier than before.
Scratch set off to find something
to eat.

A boy was swabbing the deck
as Scratch padded past. Scratch
almost got a faceful of sudsy
water.

'Look out, cat!' the boy yelled.

'Shouldn't you be below decks catching mice?'

'Watch who you're mopping, furball!' Scratch hissed back.

'Hiss at me, would you?' said the boy, and he shook his mop in Scratch's face.

Scratch leapt out of the way and grabbed onto one of the ropes that held the main mast steady. The boy shook his mop at Scratch again.

Scratch scrambled upwards. Before he knew it, he was high on the first yardarm above the mainsail. Below him the deck tilted slowly up and then slowly down again.

Scratch swayed dizzily, shook his head, and kept climbing. He was now so high above the deck that the boy with the mop looked like a toy. Scratch felt even dizzier. He wanted to hold on, but the yardarm was so smooth and hard that he couldn't get his claws into it. So he dragged himself along the yard until he came to a sailor.

'Hello,' the sailor cried. 'What are you doing up here?'

Scratch jumped onto the sailor's shoulder and held on tight. The sailor didn't like having his shoulders clawed. He yelled and waved his arms to shake Scratch loose.

Scratch held on as hard as he could. The sailor shook harder.

Suddenly Scratch was falling. He yowled as he plummeted downwards. The ship tilted, and below him was nothing but water. He shut his eyes tight, bracing himself for the splash. Then he opened one eye to see how close the water was.

Just then the ship started to lean the other way. The ship's rail was tilting towards him. Scratch reached out his paws and stretched his magnificent claws. At the last moment he hooked his claws into the rail and hung on for dear life.

He clung there shaking, ears flat to his skull. Sea spray drenched his scruffy fur. Then a rough hand grabbed him.

'Steady there, cat! You nearly took a swim!' It was the boy with the mop. He set Scratch down on the deck. 'If you want to stay alive,' he said, 'you should stay away from the sails and make yourself useful.'

Scratch scuttled to his lifeboat to wash the salt from his fur and calm his trembling paws. Staying on board was going to be harder than he thought. For a start, he had to stay clear of swinging choppers, mops and high masts. Now he had to make himself useful, too.

# 4.

# Scratch Makes Himself Useful

As soon as Scratch stopped shaking he set out to make himself useful. He would catch a mouse. That's what Maa had said cats should do. But he wished he had listened better to Maa's lessons.

At least he knew what mice smelt like, and there was the smell of many mice on board the *Silk'n'Spice*.

Especially below decks. Scratch
climbed down a hatch and
prowled along a dark passageway.
The smell of mouse got stronger and
stronger until Scratch found a tiny
hole in the wall. He stopped and
crouched beside it. The tip of his
tail twitched as he tried to remember
the rules.

'Listen, pounce, watch, wait,' he repeated to himself. But that didn't sound right. 'Pounce, wait, listen, watch.'

But listen to what? Watch where? And what was he to wait for?

Suddenly a sharp nose appeared in the hole. It was followed by some twitching whiskers, shiny black eyes and grey ears. A scrawny mouse crept out and looked around.

Scratch pounced. The mouse scuttled away between Scratch's paws and ran along the passage.

'Come back here!' wailed Scratch.

The mouse scuttled faster. Scratch chased and pounced on the mouse's tail.

The mouse turned and bit Scratch's paw. Scratch let go and the mouse scampered away.

Scratch licked his sore paw. He felt like crying. He had followed the rules. He had waited and looked and pounced.

But it hadn't worked. Maa made it look so easy, but what if he never learnt how to do it? He'd starve. Or be tossed overboard.

Scratch went back to the hole to try again. He sat and waited. He watched and listened. At last he heard a tiny scuffling. Twitching his ears, he waited until he saw a small movement. He crouched, perfectly still. And suddenly he pounced.

It was just a scrawny old mouse. But it was a good start. Scratch padded with it all the way to the galley. He wanted to show Peg-leg he could be just as useful as Fluffy.

But there was no one in the galley. Just the sound of loud snoring. The noise came from Peg-leg's cabin, where Peg-leg was taking a nap in his berth. Scratch crept in. If he was careful, he could put the mouse on the pillow where Peg-leg would see it when he woke.

Making as little sound as possible, he jumped onto the foot of the berth. Peg-leg snored on. Scratch crept along the edge of the berth and placed the mouse on the pillow.

Peg-leg's snoring sounded a like Paa's purr, only louder. His ginger beard was the colour of Maa's fur, only dirtier. The snoring and beard made Scratch think of home and his warm purring family. Peg-leg's shoulder felt warm and safe, just like Maa. Scratch closed his eyes and snuggled against Peg-leg's beard. He gave it a little pat and licked it.

Peg-leg woke with a snort.

'What the blazes!' he yelled. 'What are you doing, slobbering all over me!'

Peg-leg knocked Scratch to the floor, then grumbled and mumbled about his disturbed sleep. He rolled onto his side and snuggled his cheek into the soft pillow.

Then he sat up with a roar. The pillow had claws and a tail!

Peg-leg picked up the mouse and looked around for Scratch. Scratch sidled towards the door.

'Is this the best you can do?' Peg-leg sneered. He climbed out of his berth and stumped across the floor to the porthole. 'Fluffy used to catch a hundred of these in a day.'

Scratch yowled in dismay as Peg-leg wrenched the porthole open and tossed the mouse into the sea.

'You'll follow that mouse,' Peg-leg growled, 'if you ever try licking my face again!'

# 5.

# Scratch Becomes a Mouser

Scratch worked tirelessly that day and the next. He chased mice on deck and below deck. He hunted them along passages and over hammocks and around boxes and bags. He tripped up busy sailors.

Every time he felt like giving up, he heard Peg-leg's voice in his head: 'Fluffy could catch a hundred of these!'

'I'm fed up with Fluffy!' thought Scratch.

Scratch caught mice in the gun room, in the sailors' mess, in the stores. He kept them in a heap in his lifeboat. His plan was to lay them all in a row on Peg-leg's berth when Peg-leg wasn't watching.

When Scratch had collected enough he began the tricky task of sneaking his catch down to Peg-leg's berth. He didn't stop until there was a line of mice from the foot of the bed to the pillow.

'That should stop him raving about his precious Fluffy!' Scratch thought. Then he sat down beside the bed, purring, to wait for thanks.

He didn't get any. When Peg-leg
stumped in for his afternoon nap and
saw the mice, all Scratch got was a
roar and a boot in the ribs.

'What are you doing, putting these
disgusting things all over my bed, you
dratted moggy?' He scooped them
up, stumped to the galley and hurled
them into the fire.

'You repulsive little fleabag! Fluffy
never left his catch lying around
for me to clean up. You should be
keelhauled. Now get out before I—'

Peg-leg aimed his wooden leg at
Scratch's rump. Scratch scampered
out.

Scratch went to curl up in his lifeboat, safely away from wooden legs, choppers and mops. He didn't understand a thing. Ship's cats had to catch mice. Fluffy had caught mice. So Scratch had caught mice too. But Peg-leg had tossed his magnificent catch away!

# 6.

# Scratch Toes the Line

The next morning the sailors had to toe the line on deck for their inspection. Scratch sat and watched.

'You too, cat!' shouted the bosun. 'You must toe the line like the rest.'

Scratch stood nervously alongside the sailors as the bosun checked each man for cleanliness and health.

But what if he didn't pass? Would he be allowed to stay on board?

'Been washing all morning, eh, cat?' said the bosun when he came to Scratch. 'You could teach these scurvy salts a thing or two about keeping clean!'

Scratch purred. At least he was shipshape.

Then the sailors had to take their medicine. On weekdays it was a mouthful of lime juice. On Saturdays, Sundays and holidays it was pickled cabbage. They had to take it to keep healthy. Some of the sailors already had pimples and wobbly teeth.

The sailors always complained.

'How would you like it if your hair and teeth fell out?' Bosun asked them.

'I'd rather be bald and toothless,' said Sam, 'than eat that cabbage stuff.'

After tasting some that fell to the deck, Scratch agreed.

Then the sailors trooped off to collect their breakfast.

'Oatmeal mush with dried beef again!' whined Jem the cabin boy.

'We asked for something different, Peg-leg!' moaned Fred. 'You promised!'

'Every morning and night we get it,' Jake grumbled.

Jake was the helmsman and stood out in the weather a lot. He was always thirsty and cross. 'We're sick of it!'

'And I'm sick of your whining every morning and night!' snarled Peg-leg. 'If you want something different, cook it yourself!'

Scratch went off to catch his own breakfast. He felt sorry for the sailors with their oatmeal stew and pickled cabbage. How much happier they'd be if they ate fresh food like he did. He wondered if he should catch fresh mice for the men's dinner. Then they would be healthy and Peg-leg would be happy, and Scratch could stay safely on board!

He went straight to the store and
brought a mouse to the galley.

'Here you are then!' he purred.
'Fresh, tasty mouse for your stew!'

He laid his catch at Peg-leg's foot.
Then he waited to see what would
happen.

Peg-leg didn't even notice. He just
stood there hacking at piles of
mouldy biscuit.

'All work and no thanks,' he grumbled. Then he started sniffling. 'My old mate Fluffy (*sniff*) never complained (*sniff*). He was my only true friend (*sniff*) ...'

Scratch miaowed. Peg-leg still didn't notice.

So Scratch thought he would just get on with it. Peg-leg could thank him later when he was in a better mood. When Peg-leg turned to wipe his nose on his sleeve, Scratch quickly picked up the mouse, jumped onto the bench and dropped it in the pot. Peg-leg didn't see a thing.

Then Scratch went back to work. Many more mice would be needed to improve the sailors' stew.

Scratch soon had another mouse. He peeped around the galley door to see if the coast was clear. Peg-leg was in his cabin, blowing his nose like a foghorn. Scratch jumped lightly to the bench and added his catch to the pot.

The next time Scratch returned, Peg-leg was back at his bench with his chopper. Scratch hid behind the door. He didn't trust Peg-leg with a chopper in his hand.

Peg-leg took a wild swing at a slab of biscuit and pieces tumbled to the floor. As he knelt to pick them up, Scratch padded to the bench, popped the mouse into the pot and left the galley without Peg-leg seeing he was there.

He caught the next mouse on the poop deck where some of the sailors slept, ready for the night watch. The mice liked chewing the sailors' clothing. Maybe they thought it tasted good.

This time, when Scratch went back to the galley, Peg-leg was sitting on a stool gulping something from a bottle.

Scratch gave Peg-leg's leg a friendly rub. '*Prrrp*?' he said.

Peg-leg just wiped his eyes with his beard and cried, 'Why didn't I stay at home, instead of running away to sea?'

Scratch gave up and put the mouse in the pot. Then he went back to his hunting.

That day the sailors ate greedily.

'Best stew we've had, Peg-leg!' said Jem.

'Great flavour for a change!' said Sam. 'How about some more?'

There was almost a smile showing through Peg-leg's beard. He served out seconds. The men asked for thirds.

Peg-leg was feeling pleased with himself and scraping the pot when he noticed some strange lumps at the bottom.

Round lumps, with claws! Odd shapes, with tails!

'No more!' he suddenly shouted.
'Bottom of the pot's burnt. Now,
clear off. I've got washing up to do.'

'That's not fair!' grumbled Sam.
'Bosun got thirds!'

'Let me scrape out the pot!'
said Jem helpfully. 'It'll save you
washing up!'

Peg-leg waved his ladle. 'I told you.
All that's left is burnt bits!'

'You always give us burnt grub,
Peg-leg!' said Jake, reaching for
the pot. 'And this burnt grub is
yummy!'

'Sorry, Jake,' said Peg-leg. 'The scrapings are for the cat. He's been earning his keep over the last few days. Caught some mice.'

Scratch pricked his ears. He was going to be rewarded at last! He crept out of hiding and rubbed against Peg-leg's stump. Peg-leg ignored him. Scratch mewed to let Peg-leg know he was there, ready for his scrapings.

When the last of the grumbling men were gone, Peg-leg suddenly grabbed Scratch and shook him.

'What are you trying to do to me?' he yelled. 'Dropping mice in the pot! Want to see me keelhauled, do you?'

Scratch tried to explain that he was only making himself useful, but Peg-leg shook him harder. Then Scratch tried to tell Peg-leg that cats didn't like being squeezed around the middle and shaken.

'Quit yowling!' said Peg-leg. 'I don't like you, cat. But it seems you can catch mice. So go ahead and catch 'em. But don't ever let me see you in my galley again, or you'll be the one flavouring the stew!'

Peg-leg dropped Scratch.

Scratch ran.

# 7.

# Scratch Makes a Friend

Scratch hovered behind the galley door with a very fat mouse. He had caught it behind the scuttlebutt and hoped it might help Peg-leg forget about cat stew.

But Peg-leg had a problem. A group of sailors stood in the galley doorway with their dinner bowls. They were throwing their dinner at him. A large blob of weevilly oatmeal landed in Peg-leg's hair. Another hit his beard.

'What's this tasteless muck?' yelled Jake.

'Why can't we have more of that stuff you served us the other day?' cried Jonas.

Voices rose in agreement.

'There's nothing else to eat,' Peg-leg shouted back. 'Mouldy oats and dried meat and dried-up taters is all we got!'

'The other day the stew was delicious,' yelled Jonas.

'What did you put in it?' asked Fred.

'Nothing. Just the usual stuff. Except . . . maybe a pinch of salt.'

'Well, matey, you'd better find
more of that fancy salt,' growled Jake.
His black beard bristled like an angry
tomcat's tail. 'We want better food or
we'll be putting you ashore on the
next deserted island.'

'Maybe we won't even wait for an
island,' Jonas growled. 'Just put you
overboard.'

Peg-leg trembled on his peg-leg.

'Alright, men,' he muttered. 'I'll put more, er, salt in the next batch. It costs a lot, but for you ...'

Peg-leg sat in the oatmeal puddle on the galley floor. He pulled at his beard, scratched his head, and groaned. Then he scraped bits of stew out of his beard. He gazed at the bench, tapped his peg-leg and drummed his foot on the floor.

Scratch cowered behind the galley door. He didn't dare move. He was sure Peg-leg was thinking about cat stew.

'Here, Kitty, Kitty,' Peg-leg hissed. 'Come to your Uncle Peg-leg!'

Scratch fluffed the fur along his back.

Peg-leg got up and clumped towards the door. 'Come here, Kitty,' he wheezed. 'Wherever you are.'

He saw Scratch peeping and made a grab for him. Scratch darted past him and tore along the passageway, leaving Peg-leg with a handful of fur from Scratch's tail.

Scratch ducked into the men's quarters. *Thud, plonk, thud, plonk.* Peg-leg followed him.

'Here, puss. There's a good cat!' he whispered.

A tiny mew of fright escaped from Scratch.

'Come out, puss. We've got a job to do!' rasped Peg-leg.

'Not likely!' thought Scratch. He fled past Peg-leg's hands, ran to the food stores and sheltered behind a barrel of dried beef.

*Thud, plonk, thud, plonk.* 'Here, kitty, kitty. Come here, drat you!'

Peg-leg searched behind boxes and on shelves. Scratch broke from his cover and bolted out of the door. This time he flew up the hatch ladder and out on deck. He scuttled about, looking for safety.

'Look at the cat!' said Fred, who was mending a sail. 'Chasing mice, I reckon.'

'Top mouser,' said Jem, who wasn't doing anything. 'Peg-leg says so.'

Scratch didn't want to be cat stew, and he didn't want to be thrown overboard. He ran to the bow of the ship, turned and ran all the way back to the stern.

*Thud, plonk, thud, plonk.* Peg-leg was getting closer. *Thud, plonk, rustle.*

Scratch froze. Peg-leg was very close. *Crash!* An upturned basket suddenly landed on Scratch. He was trapped.

'Gotcha!' said Peg-leg.

Scratch fought and growled. He mewed and howled. But Peg-leg reached under the basket, grabbed him and held on tight.

'Now listen here, moggy,' he said. 'I'll make a deal. You keep catching those mice, eh? And then you give them to me.'

Scratch tried to bite Peg-leg's hand.

Peg-leg gripped tighter. 'But it's our little secret,' he said. 'No one must know. If I get caught putting mice in the stew, I'll be thrown overboard. And if that happens, I'll take you with me as quick as you can say miaow!'

Peg-leg tucked Scratch under his arm and took him down to the galley. He slammed the door shut and lifted the cat to the beam above the bench. 'There you go, cat. A top mouser gets the Top Spot. But you'll have to work hard. Our lives depend on it.'

Scratch was amazed. 'He's given me the Top Spot,' Scratch thought to himself. He gazed around. It certainly was the top spot. He could see everything in the galley, and even through to the sailors' mess. He dug his claws into the beam for a big scratch. A cloud of splinters, dust and fur floated onto the bench below.

'Oy! Fluffy never dropped fluff in my cooking!' Peg-leg roared. 'Now, get out and earn your place in the Top Spot!'

So Scratch started catching mice for Peg-leg's stew. He left his catch beside the bench, and Peg-leg popped them into the stew. Just before each meal was served, he fished the mice back out and put them in a bowl for Scratch.

The men were happy.

'Who'd have thought it,' said Fred. 'Just a pinch of salt makes that much difference!'

Peg-leg became almost friendly. He told everyone that Scratch was shaping up to be a top mouser.

Scratch didn't have to hide in the lifeboat any more. He spent his breaks sleeping in the Top Spot. Best of all, Peg-leg didn't mention Fluffy more than once a day.

# 8.

# Scratch, Peg-leg and the Cat

Some days later the sailors sat nursing their full tummies. Scratch sat purring in the Top Spot.

'Good stew tonight, Peg-leg!' grinned Jonas.

'Great flavour,' said Jake. 'Keep it coming, Peg-leg.'

Suddenly there was a howl from the captain's cabin.

'Oh, my giddy aunt!' the captain screeched. 'What's this?'

He lurched into the galley. He was holding a mouse by its tail, dripping gravy. The sailors gasped. Peg-leg's jaw dropped.

'Peg-leg, are you trying to kill me?' The captain let the mouse fall to the floor. He pulled a purple spotted handkerchief from his pocket and wiped each finger and then his mouth.

'Well, Captain, sir ...' Peg-leg stammered. 'The cat must have ...'

'You scurvy twit!' the captain cried, smoothing his jacket. 'There's a mouse in my stew and you're blaming the cat! What you need is a *taste* of the cat!'

Scratch flattened his ears. His fur
bristled. Did the captain want to put
him in the pot?

'Please, Captain, sir! Not the cat!'
Peg-leg cried. 'Anything but the cat!'

Scratch blinked gratefully. Peg-leg
would protect him!

'Yes, the cat!' the captain yelled.
'Take him up, Jake and Jonas!'

'I never did it!' Peg-leg cried again.
'I don't want to taste the cat!'

Scratch tried to look invisible.

Jake and Jonas grabbed Peg-leg
by the arms and dragged him up
on deck. The rest of the men
crowded after them. They shoved
and pushed and got stuck in the
doorway.

'You don't need to see this, Jem,'
said Fred. 'You stay here.'

'Please, Fred,' said Jem. 'I have to
watch if I'm to become an old salt
like you.'

Scratch thought maybe he should
find out what was happening if he,
too, was to become an old salt like
Fred. But he would have watch from

a safe hiding spot. He didn't want Peg-leg tasting him!

He crept out of the galley and up on deck, then slunk to his lifeboat.

The sailors had lined up on the deck. 'The cat! The cat!' they yelled.

'No! Not the cat!' cried Peg-leg.

Scratch squirmed under a canvas and lay as still as he could.

The captain arrived with a brown leather bag. He had taken off his jacket and looked splendid in his white ruffled shirt. The buttons on his jacket gleamed in the sun and his stylish glossy ponytail bobbed in the breeze. The captain pulled something out of his bag.

Peg-leg groaned and fell over. Jake hauled him back to his feet.

The men shouted.

'This isn't fair!' whispered Jem.

'A sailor's life ain't fair!' answered Fred.

'There are mice all over the ship!' said Jem. 'One might have fallen in by mistake.'

'Cook should keep a cleaner galley,' said Fred.

'Not the cat-o'-nine-tails!' cried Peg-leg. 'Not the whip!'

Scratch peeped from his hiding place. Did Peg-leg say a whip?

The captain had a long frayed rope in his hand. The rope had nine thinner ropes attached at one end. He held it up and swished its tail.

Scratch climbed out of his hiding place and crept closer. He wasn't going to be made into stew after all. When they spoke of the cat, they hadn't been talking about Scratch, they'd been talking about a whip. The cat-o'-nine-tails.

'It wasn't me, I swear!' Peg-leg whined. 'I never put no mouse in the pot!'

The captain rolled up his frilly sleeves.

'It was the kitten,' Peg-leg said. 'You should give *him* a taste of the cat! Filthy little beast, with his fleas and his fur and his dead mice, and taking Fluffy's Top Spot.'

Scratch couldn't believe his ears.

'Fluffy?' said the captain. 'The one I threw overboard for stealing?'

The men growled and muttered.

'Whipping is too good for you,' the captain went on. 'Fancy blaming a little kitten! I think you should follow Fluffy overboard!'

'Then the kitten comes with me!' Peg-leg howled.

'No he doesn't!' The captain scooped Scratch into his arms and tickled his ears. 'From now on, this little ball of ginger fluff is going to live in my cabin. He will stay there where no one can harm a hair on his fuzzy-wuzzy little head. He will be the Number One Ship's Cat and I shall name him Pussykins.'

# How It Ended

It was 'Pussykins' that did it. And Peg-leg's long sad face.

After all, Scratch really had caught the mice for the stew. It was partly his fault. And Scratch had to admit that he and Peg-leg *had* become friends. Sort of.

'Will I ever see land again?' Peg-leg moaned.

Scratch dug his claws into the seat
of the tiny dinghy. He sharpened
them and glared at Peg-leg. Friend or
not, Peg-leg was still a grizzler.

'Why did I do it?' Scratch
wondered. 'Was I crazy?'

All his dreams had been about to come true. He was about to become the captain's number one ship's cat. There was no better job on the high seas! But he had changed his mind just as Peg-leg was lowered overboard. Maybe he was crazy … but it was better than being called a *sweet ickle fuzzy-wuzzy kitty cat*!

'I'd give my good leg for the sight of a ship,' moaned Peg-leg. 'Or the sound of a ship's bell!'

Scratch turned and gazed at the black sail on the horizon. It had been coming closer all morning. Its black flag was decorated with a white skull and bones.

Rescue was on its way!

Or was it?

# Words Sailors Use

| | |
|---|---|
| aloft | above the deck of the ship, perhaps in the rigging |
| berth | a bunk bed on a ship |
| the bosun | the sailor in charge of the ship's crew |
| bow | the forward part of a ship |
| cat-o'-nine-tails/ the cat | a whip, used to punish sailors |
| dock | an area of calm water in a harbour where ships are moored |
| galley | a ship's kitchen |
| gangway | the part of a ship's side where passengers and crew get on and off the ship |
| hatch | an opening in the ship's deck, covered by a watertight lid |
| helmsman | the sailor who steers the ship |
| keelhaul | to drag a sailor through the sea, beneath the bottom of a ship, as a punishment |
| mainsail | the most important sail on a sailing ship, raised from the main mast |
| mast | a stout pole rising straight up from the deck of a ship, which supports the yards and sails |
| old salt | an experienced sailor |
| poop deck | the roof of the poop cabin, which is found at the back of a ship |

| | |
|---|---|
| porthole | a window in the side of a ship, sometimes round in shape |
| quarters | the living areas on board a ship |
| sailors' mess | the living quarters of a ship's crew |
| scupper | a drain hole on the deck |
| scurvy | an illness. Olden-day sailors often suffered from scurvy on long voyages because they could not store fresh food. To call another sailor "scurvy" was an insult. |
| scuttlebutt | a water barrel on a ship, with a hole cut out, into which a sailor could dip his drinking cup |
| setting sails | to unroll and expand the sails, in order to get ready to start a journey |
| ship's biscuit | crackers used during long sea voyages. They kept for years because they were very hard. |
| shipshape | in good order, tidy and well-arranged |
| stern | the back part of the ship |
| toe the line | When the bosun called the sailors for inspection, the men had to line up with the tips of their toes touching a line painted on the deck. |
| weevilly | infected with weevils. Weevils are beetles, seen as pests on board a ship because they destroy stores of food. |
| yardarm | either end of a yard of a square sail. A "yard" is the name given to the wooden post attached cross-ways to the mast, from which the sail is hung. |

# About the Author

Jessica Green has always loved cats, and shares her home with four furry feline friends—Fang, Felis, Tre and Tumnus. She has never had a cat quite like Scratch, but she once had a mad little three-legged cat called Gilbert who used to get into all kinds of strife.

Jessica learned a lot about life at sea when she tried sailing with her husband in his yacht. She soon realised that she hated being cold and wet, falling overboard, and being shouted at!

# About the Artist

Mitch Vane would love to run away to sea but she can't because after half an hour on a boat she gets seasick!

Mitch once had a cat called George. He was a lot like Scratch and liked to sit on the newspaper when Mitch was trying to read it!

Nowadays Mitch has a cat called Patchy. Mitch and her family love Patchy a lot, but not when she leaps up and down the hall at three in the morning.

For more exciting adventures
on the high seas with

# SCRATCH KITTEN

look out for the second adventure ...

# SCRATCH KITTEN
## on the
# PIRATE'S SHOULDER

# How The Next Book Starts . . .

Scratch and Peg-leg had been cast
adrift because they'd put a mouse in
the captain's stew. Now they were
alone on the ocean in a tiny dinghy.
The sun shone hot and no breeze
blew. But now, at last, rescue was
at hand.

Scratch teetered on the side of the
boat as he watched a ship with black

sails draw closer. He swished his tail. It was the closest thing he had to a flag.

'Shiver my whiskers,' he yowled. 'We're saved!'

Scratch was so excited he didn't notice the ship was a leaky, shabby old tub. He didn't care that its sails were black, or that the mainsail had a picture of a white skull wearing an eye patch.

But Peg-leg covered his eyes and screeched.

The ship drew alongside, towering above the dinghy like a shark over a fish. Men hung over the railing and shouted. A man with a long, tousled braid of hair threw down a rope.

It tangled around Peg-leg's feet so that he fell over. The sailors laughed, but Scratch wasted no time on Peg-leg. He leapt at the rope, clawed his way up it and jumped aboard ...

# Acknowledgements

Thanks to Michael, for trying, and failing,
to teach me to love the water.

Thanks to Nick, Richard and Gillian,
for assuring me that writing about mad
kittens is far more useful than a tidy house.

Thanks to Mitch, for seeing Scratch
so clearly.

Special thanks to Margrete, for planting the
idea of Scratch into my mind.

*Jessica*